Turtles In My Sandbox

by Jennifer Keats Curtis   Illustrated by Emanuel Schongut

Early one morning in June, Mama Turtle —a diamondback terrapin—silently swam along the bay's shore. Now and then, her head poked above the cool waves. Below the water, her webbed feet moved quickly. Her belly was full of eggs. She wanted to lay those eggs on the beach close to where she had been born.

Mama Turtle swam toward the shoreline. After checking for animals that might hurt her, she used her sharp black claws to pull herself out of the water and onto the muddy bank.

Mama pulled her round body over the slippery slope and up the steep bank. Her lower shell scraped the stubby grass as she made her way onto her nesting ground—the sand.

Using her strong back feet, she dug a teardrop-shaped hole by scooping the sand. First she used her right foot, then her left. She laid 10 pinkish-white, leathery eggs. Then using that same right-left motion, she covered the small eggs with sand.

Mama Turtle had done her best to hide her nest. She ambled back down the slope and slipped back into the bay. The only sign that she had been there were her funny-looking footprints.

Early the next morning, a curious, curly-haired girl found those eggs in an odd place—her old sandbox! As it turned out, Mama Turtle hadn't been on the beach at all. She had been in Maggie's sandbox!

Maggie had seen lots of eggs before—in birds' nests and in egg cartons. But she had never found any in her sandbox. At first, she didn't realize what they were. Then she looked closely at the tracks leading up to the nest. They looked like the letter "J" on both sides of a wider line in the sand. She realized they were turtle footprints.

"Mom," Maggie called, "you're not going to believe what's in my sandbox!"

Maggie did not know much about baby turtles. She and her mom visited the aquarium and the zoo. They looked up websites. Finally, they called the Turtle Lady to ask what terrapins eat, when they sleep, or whether they would make good pets.

"Why was that turtle in my sandbox?" Maggie asked the Turtle Lady.

"Mama Turtle thought it was the beach," explained the Turtle Lady. "She was lucky. Sometimes turtles and other animals can't come ashore at all. People put up rocks or bulkheads so their beaches won't get washed away."

Maggie was happy that Mama Turtle had found a safe place to lay her eggs. But Maggie worried that other terrapins might not be so lucky. The Turtle Lady assured Maggie that she was just one of many people helping terrapins. She talked about a turtle-sitting program. Turtle sitters feed and protect the teeny hatchlings to give them a "head-start." Sitters help the babies until they are big enough to fend for themselves in the wild.

Maggie wanted to be a turtle sitter. She and her mom placed a wire nest protector over the eggs. This would help keep animals, like raccoons, from eating the eggs. She was excited that baby turtles were coming.

Every day that summer, Maggie read about turtles. After 55 days, she began checking the nest. Had any hatchlings come out of the eggs?

One hot September day, as Maggie sat by her sandbox, she noticed a little dent in the top of the nest. She carefully brushed off the top layer of sand so she could see into the nest. As she watched, an egg wobbled. A small grey and black foot popped right through the shell. The hatchling's grey and white speckled face followed. The newborn's small egg tooth helped it break through the egg. Then nothing happened. The baby was resting. As Maggie watched, another grey and black foot burst through the shell. Within an hour, the whole turtle had worked its way out of the egg.

Maggie thought the tiny turtle was beautiful. She gently touched his soft, top shell (carapace). She admired the 13 raised ridges (scutes) on his back. Then she gently flipped him over. The sticky, light yellow egg sac was still attached to his belly. Maggie saw pretty, black markings on his bottom shell (plastron).

"Hold still so I can look at you," Maggie giggled to the squirmy turtle. She named him Scamp. As Maggie stared at Scamp, she suddenly realized why the terrapins are called diamondbacks. The dark marks on the turtle's back look like snail shells. They spiral around, becoming smaller and smaller. "It's like looking into a sparkly diamond!" she cried.

Maggie marveled over Scamp's scutes. Then she realized that other eggs were hatching too. "Mom, come quick!" she yelled. Together they watched eight more turtles break out of their eggs. One by one, Maggie named them.

Freckles' skin was covered with little black spots, which of course, looked a lot like freckles.

Tudo was pale yellow. He hardly had any spots at all.

Popper popped right out of his shell.

Poky seemed to take forever.

Terpy was the biggest turtle to be born.

Scooter was the fastest.

Shelly had trouble getting a piece of egg off her head.

Junior, the last terrapin to hatch, was a surprise. His whole head was grey!

One egg did not hatch. Maggie covered it and left it in the sandy nest covered by sand and the nest protector.

Maggie and her mom had learned that new babies stay in their nest for a few days and survive on the sticky yolk left in the egg. After that, they need fresh water and real food.

As part of the "head-start" program, Maggie's turtles would eat cut-up little fish and turtle pellets. They would also live in tanks.

Maggie and her mom set up three tanks with heat lamps. Each tank contained slightly salty water, like the bay water. In the wild, terrapins rarely wander far from the water—except to lay eggs in the spring and early summer. But they do like to climb up and rest or bask on floating logs or on rocks near the water's edge. Maggie placed small stones and a few big sticks in the tanks to help the turtles feel at home.

It was too early to tell if the turtles were boys or girls so Maggie placed them into the tanks by hatch order. Scamp, Freckles, and Tudo went into one tank. Popper, Poky, and Terpy went into the second. Scooter, Shelly, and Junior shared the third tank.

As the babies grew, Maggie learned that each turtle was very different. But they all wore big grins made by their small beaks.

Poky and Popper looked like twins. They were exactly the same size. Both had two tiny black markings right between their eyes and their nostrils. She could tell them apart because Poky would shyly pull his head down, almost into his shell when Maggie approached the tank. Popper wasn't shy at all. He grinned up at Maggie every time she went near him.

Every morning, Maggie turned on the heat lamps. Then she fed the turtles. She loved watching them. Freckles zipped through the water and darted at the food. Popper really lived up to his name. He popped out of the water every time she got near the tank. He would practically leap out of the water when she walked near him, as if he knew she was coming to feed him. What a hungry turtle!

At night, Maggie turned off all the lights. She fed the turtles again, mostly cut-up fish. Sometimes Maggie gave them a "fishcicle," a Popsicle made out of frozen minnows! Sometimes the turtles ate small snails called periwinkles. Junior loved soft clams and razor clams. Poky enjoyed eating the roots of marsh plants; but he always ate slowly. Scamp's favorite food was worms.

Maggie fed the turtles the kind of food they would have eaten in the wild. She cleaned the tanks every other week, and made sure they had plenty of light.

The lucky turtles stayed well fed and warm under their heat lamps all winter. In the bay, terrapins hibernate during the winter months. Even new hatchlings bury themselves in the sand near the shore. They sleep until warmer weather arrives. However, Maggie's "head-started" turtles ate—and grew—while the wild terrapins slept. By the following June, all of the terrapins, except Junior, were bigger than any hibernating turtles. Since Maggie's turtles were as large as the palm of her hand, she knew they were big enough to release.

On the first day of summer, Maggie and her mom joined the Turtle Lady and wildlife experts to free the terrapins in the bay. They were not far from where Mama had laid her eggs in Maggie's sandbox the year before.

Maggie helped the experts place metal tags through the edges of the shell (marginal scutes) of each turtle. The tags didn't hurt the turtles but could possibly help the experts learn more about the turtles.

After all the turtles were tagged, Maggie placed them on the sand. She watched them race to the water's edge and drop into the bay. Poky was last—of course!

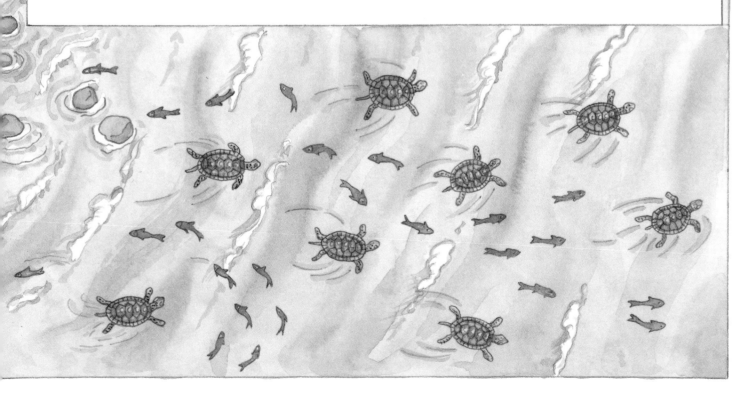

Maggie stared as the nine-month-old diamondbacks swam away. After a few minutes of freedom, they popped their heads above the waves as if to see how far they were from the shore. As they dipped below the surface again, each waved "good-bye" with a back foot before disappearing again. Maggie waved back.

For Creative Minds

Diamond Terrapin Fun Facts

The word terrapin comes from the Algonquian Indian word *torope*, which means "edible turtle that lives in the brackish water."

Diamondback terrapins are named for the diamond-shaped rings that appear on their top shells (carapace).

Female terrapins are much bigger than the males.

Webbed feet help them swim in the water, and the claws help them pull themselves on the shore.

Terrapins can pull their heads and legs into their bodies for protection. They don't close up completely like a box turtle.

Turtles do not have teeth; they do have strong enough beaks or jaws to bite through shells.

Head-started terrapins usually eat turtle pellets, but their diets can include cut-up worms, snails, and other foods that they would eat in their natural habitat.

In the wild, diamondback terrapins eat periwinkles (snails), clams, crabs, and some marsh plants.

Diamondback Terrapin Life Cycle

Put the diamondback terrapin life-cycle events in order to spell the scrambled word.

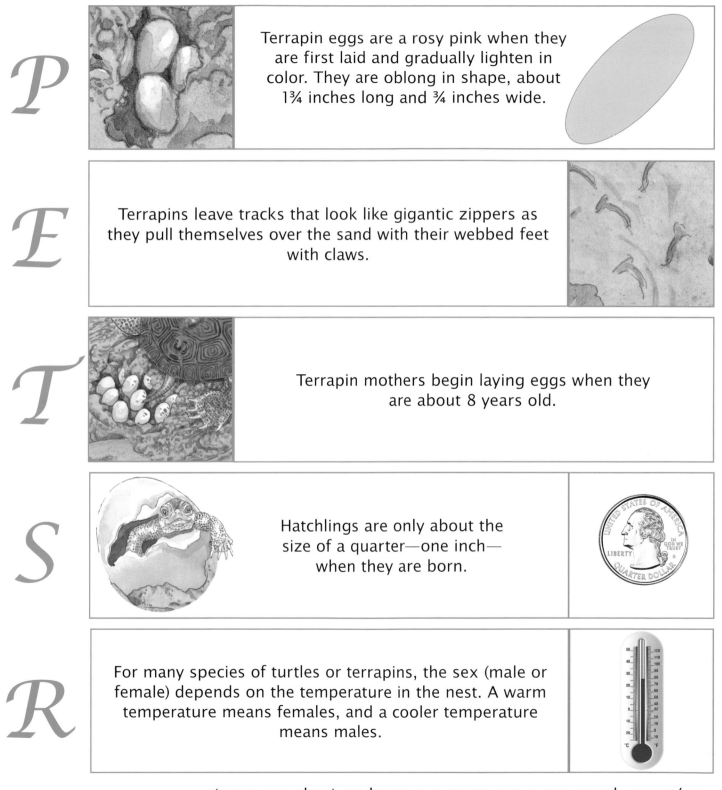

P — Terrapin eggs are a rosy pink when they are first laid and gradually lighten in color. They are oblong in shape, about 1¾ inches long and ¾ inches wide.

E — Terrapins leave tracks that look like gigantic zippers as they pull themselves over the sand with their webbed feet with claws.

T — Terrapin mothers begin laying eggs when they are about 8 years old.

S — Hatchlings are only about the size of a quarter—one inch—when they are born.

R — For many species of turtles or terrapins, the sex (male or female) depends on the temperature in the nest. A warm temperature means females, and a cooler temperature means males.

Answer: TERPS: Diamondback terrapins are Maryland's state reptile. The University of Maryland's sports teams are called the Terrapins (Terps for short).

Diamondback terrapins are found in the brackish (somewhat salty) waters of the Atlantic and Gulf coasts, from Massachusetts to Florida and westward to the Texas and Mexican border (shown by the yellow line on the map below).

They live in bays, lagoons, rivers, and marshes. Experts believe that diamondbacks are the only turtles in North America that live entirely in brackish water.

In what states might you find diamondback terrapins?

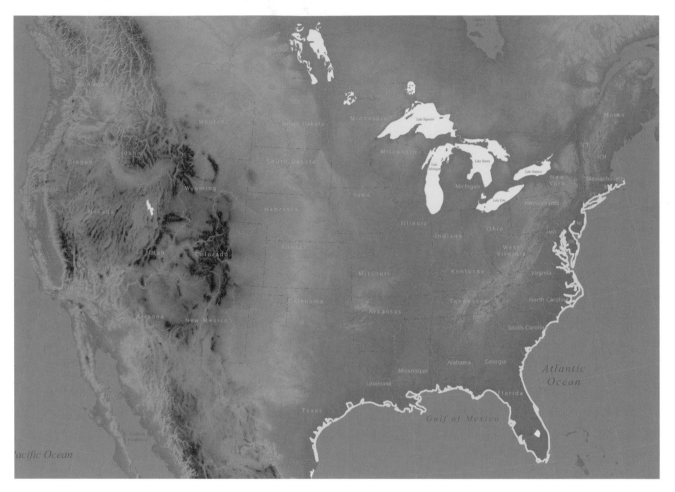

Diamondback terrapins used to be very common, but their numbers have declined in some areas. They are even considered endangered (at risk of disappearing from the earth) or threatened (at risk of becoming endangered) in some states.

To help protect them, some states now limit fishing or prohibit trapping and selling terrapins for food. In some areas, you might even see a "slow: terrapin crossing" sign along the road. This is to tell drivers to be aware, because terrapins may have to cross roads to get to nesting areas and are often hit by cars.

When roads, houses, and other buildings are built along the coast and in salt-marshes, terrapin nesting areas are lost.

Diamondback Terrapin Craft

Copy or download the page and color the turtle. (Do not cut or color the turtle in the book!) Cut out along the heavy black lines and cut along the heavy lines for the "darts" – see arrows. Fold the "dart" area so that the grey is hidden and tape or glue shut. See smaller illustration for reference.

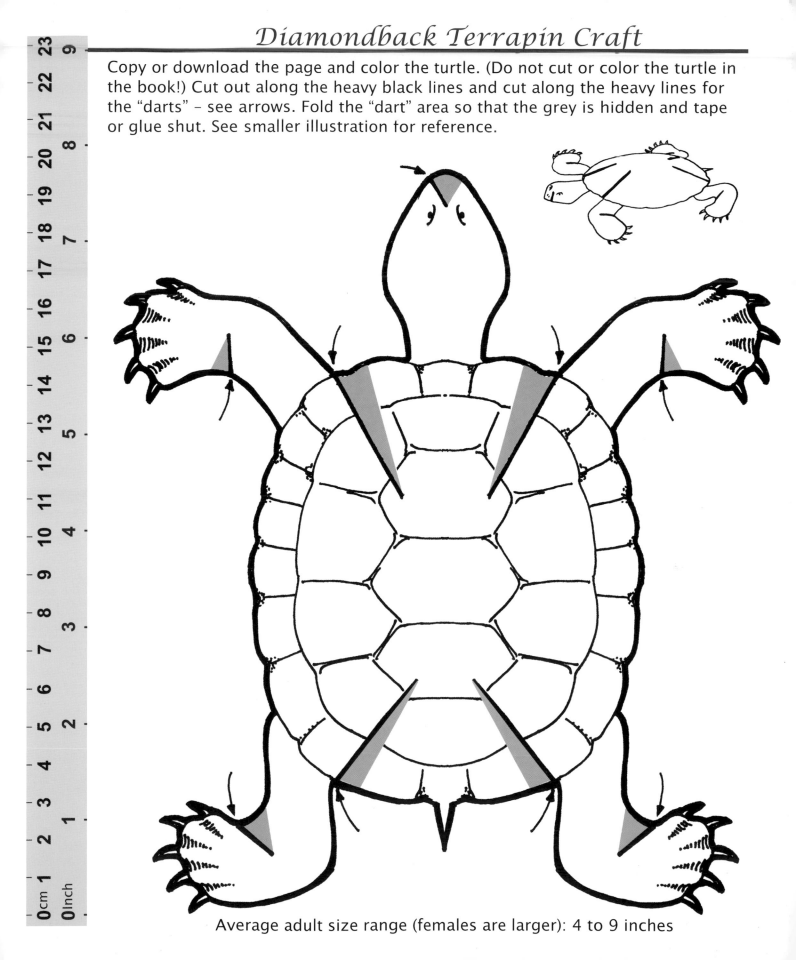

Average adult size range (females are larger): 4 to 9 inches

This story is based on an actual program that allows students in Maryland to help wildlife experts protect and learn more about their state reptile—the diamondback terrapin. Terrapin Station was started by a woman affectionately known as Maryland's Turtle Lady, Marguerite Whilden. This program is sponsored by a cooperative of private and public organizations; the Terrapin Institute, the Maryland State Department of Education (MSDE), Maryland's Department of Natural Resources (DNR), the University of Maryland Biotechnology (UMBI), and the author of this book. To learn more, see www.terrapinbook.com. In addition, the Philadelphia Zoo and the Wetlands Institute in New Jersey in cooperation with The Richard Stockton College of New Jersey, provide other programs to support and care for diamondback terrapins. Individual schools from Florida to Massachusetts have student projects to help terrapins or to monitor their nests.

The author donates a percentage of her royalties from this book to the Terrapin Institute.

Thanks to Jeff Popp, of the Terrapin Institute; Willem M. Roosenburg, Department of Biological Sciences at Ohio University and Joseph A. Butler, Department of Biology at the University of North Florida, co-chairs of the Diamondback Terrapin Working Group; and to Mary B. Hollinger, Oceanographer at NOAA for reviewing the accuracy of this book.

Publisher's Cataloging-In-Publication Data
Curtis, Jennifer Keats.
Turtles in my sandbox / by Jennifer Keats Curtis ; illustrated by Emanuel Schongut.
p. : ill. (chiefly col.) ; cm.

[32] p. : col. ill. ; cm.

Summary: Maggie finds turtle eggs in her sandbox and decides to become a "turtle sitter" to help the baby diamondback terrapins. She watches them hatch and then raises them until they are big enough to fend for themselves. Includes "For Creative Minds" section with terrapin fun facts and turtle habitat crafts.

ISBN: 978-0-9768823-74 (hardcover)
ISBN: 978-1-6071811-94 (pbk.)
Also available as an eBook featuring auto-flip, auto-read, 3D-page-curling, and selectable English and Spanish text and audio
Interest level: 4-8
Grade level: P-3
Lexile Level: 770 Lexile Code: AD

1. Turtles--Juvenile fiction. 2. Turtles--Fiction. I. Schongut, Emanuel. II. Title.

PZ7.C87 Tur 2006
[Fic]   2006924846

Manufactured in China, January, 2010
This product conforms to CPSIA 2008
Second Printing

Sylvan Dell Publishing
976 Houston Northcutt Blvd., Suite 3
Mt. Pleasant, SC 29464